BIG
LITTLE CRITTER® BOOK

ON THE GO

BY GINA AND MERCER MAYER

Manufactured in the United States by Courier Corporation
46983401 2013

Published by FastPencil PREMIERE
307 Orchard City Drive, Suite 210, Campbell CA 95008
Premiere.FastPencil.com

JUST A BAD DAY

BY GINA AND MERCER MAYER

When I woke up this morning, it was raining.
I knew it was going to be a bad day.

I wanted a bowl of Sugar Krispies
for breakfast, but the box was empty.
I had to have oatmeal instead. Yuck!

I looked for my favorite shirt, but it was dirty. I had to wear a shirt I didn't even like.

I wanted to watch cartoons on TV, but they were all reruns.
This really was a bad day.

So I decided to paint a picture. But my sister had left the tops off my paints, and they were all dried up.

I wanted to play with my new truck, but my dad had stepped on it by accident and broken the wheel.

So I decided to put my puzzle together instead.
Some of the pieces were missing.
This was such a bad day.

I asked Mom if I could play in the rain. But she said, "It's too wet."

So I let the dog in to play. But Mom made me put him back out because he was too wet.

15

I said, "But I'm bored."
Mom said, "Why don't you play a game with your sister?"

I tried to play cards with my sister.
She threw them all over the room.

Then we played chase, but Mom made us stop
because we were too noisy.
"Please play something that's a little more
quiet," Mom said.

So we colored in our coloring book. I got mad at my sister because she broke some of my crayons.
She cried. Mom yelled at both of us.
Boy! Was this a bad day!

21

Then it stopped raining. But Mom wouldn't let me go outside because it was so muddy.

And my baseball game was canceled because
the field was too wet.
This was the worst day ever.

Then my dad came home. He had a
surprise for me. It was a truck, just
like the one he had broken.
He brought my sister a surprise, too.

25

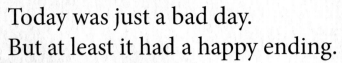

Today was just a bad day.
But at least it had a happy ending.

JUST AN AIRPLANE

BY GINA AND MERCER MAYER

We went on a trip. We had to fly on an airplane. My sister and I were excited—we had never been on an airplane before.

We left early the morning of the trip
so we'd have plenty of time. We didn't
want the plane to leave without us.

It was a good thing we left early.
There was lots of traffic.

By the time we got to the airport, it was almost time for our plane to take off. We had to run all the way through the airport.

But it was okay because our plane
was late, too.

We had time for breakfast, so we ate
at a restaurant with big windows.
We watched planes taking off and landing.
Then it was time to board our plane.

35

When we got to our gate, they were just calling our flight. They let us go on first because we had a baby.

Mom and Dad and the baby sat together.
My sister and I sat across the aisle.
We got our seat belts all tangled up.

Then the plane started moving.
It was really slow at first,
but it got faster and faster.
Then it took off into the sky.

As the plane climbed, my ears felt weird.
There were clouds right outside of the window.
And everything on the ground looked so tiny.

I guess my baby brother's ears felt weird, too.
He started crying.

He cried when we were having our lunch.

He cried through the movie.

He cried when Dad walked around with him.

When it was almost time to land, the baby
fell asleep. I think everyone was glad.

When the plane landed, it made a screeching sound. It was speeding fast down the runway. Then the plane slowed down and the pilot parked it at the gate—just like a car.

As we were leaving the plane, the flight attendant asked, "Would you like to see the cockpit and meet the crew?" Mom and Dad said we could.

We met the pilot and the copilot and
the navigator. They let us sit in their seats
and try on their hats. The pilot gave us
coloring books to keep.

Then it was time to get off the plane. Mom and Dad were ready to leave, but I wasn't. I wanted to ride in the plane again!

Mom said, "Don't worry, we have to
take a plane to get home.

Going on a trip is fun, but flying
in an airplane is the most fun of all.

JUST ME AND MY BICYCLE

BY GINA AND MERCER MAYER

I have a really cool bicycle.
It's shiny and red and almost
as big as me.

Dad said, "You have to take
good care of a nice bicycle like this."
I said I would.

So I always keep it clean and shiny—
well, almost always.

And I put it in the garage every night.
If I forget, I have to go out in the dark
to put it away. That helps me remember.

My bike takes me everywhere
I want to go. As long as it's not
across the street.

My bike and I have lots of adventures
together.
When I'm a spy, we hide in the bushes
gathering top secret information.
Then we ride at top speed to our
headquarters. We never get caught.

When I'm a policeman, my bike is my motorcycle. We speed around chasing bad guys. We always catch them.

When I am a cowboy, my bike is
my bucking bronco. But it never
throws me off.

Today my friends came over to my house.
We played on our bikes. We made a
bridge over the ditch in the backyard.
We had a lot of fun riding over it.
Until it broke.

Then we took turns pulling each other
in the wagon. Mom made us stop
because we might get hurt.

After my friends went home,
I asked Mom and Dad to go
on a bike ride with me.

My sister sat in a special seat on Mom's bike. She doesn't have a big bike because her legs are too short to reach the pedals.

We rode all over town. We even rode across the street. Mom and Dad got tired, but I didn't.

Then we stopped and had an ice cream cone.
I wanted to ride my bike while I ate my cone,
but Mom said, "Sit down."

On the way home I hit a big bump.
I fell off my bike and hurt my knee.
It started bleeding. That made me cry.

Dad gave me a hug and said
it would be okay. He wanted me
to get back on my bike.

I said no. I was mad at my bike for making me fall. I even kicked it. Mom said, "It's not the bike's fault you fell. It was just an accident."

I wasn't so sure, but I got back on my bike
and we rode home. I didn't fall anymore.
I guess Mom was right.

When we got home, my sister wanted to ride
my bike. My dad sat her on it and pushed her
around the driveway. Then my dad went to buy
helmets for the whole family—just in case.

When my sister's legs get longer, maybe she will have a big bike, too. Then I can show her how to take care of it.

She might even be lucky enough
to get a bike as good as mine—
well, almost as good.

GOING TO THE RACES

BY GINA AND MERCER MAYER

My uncle is a race car driver. He asked if I wanted to go to the races with him. Dad said I could.

The race car was up on a trailer.
I thought we were going to drive
the car to the racetrack. Instead,
we rode in the front of the van
with my aunt.

When we got to the racetrack,
my uncle put on his racing suit.
It was the same colors as his car.

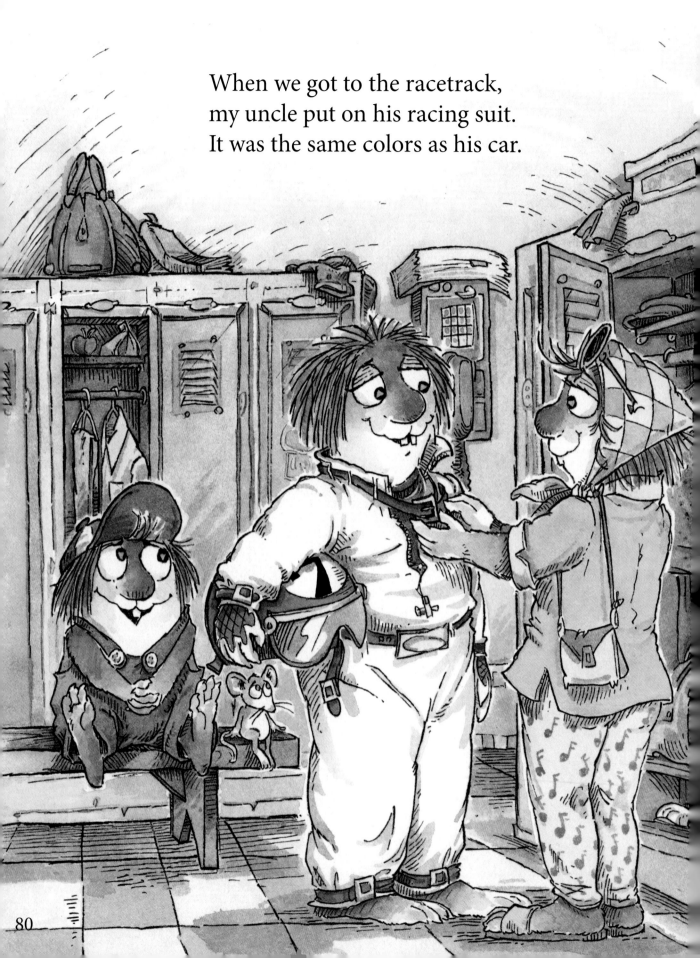

He let me try on his helmet.
It was too big.

During the warm-up, my uncle
drove me around the track in his car.
We went fast, but not too fast.

Then the race started. I sat in the
stands with my aunt. She bought me
a hot dog and some popcorn.

The race cars were really loud.
My ears hurt.

My aunt and I cheered for my uncle
every time he passed by. He was
ahead of the other cars.

Then another car hit my uncle's car
and made it spin.

The yellow warning flag was waved.
The other cars had to slow down so they
wouldn't hit my uncle's car, too.

The pit critters checked my uncle's car.
When they said it was okay, he got back
in the race. He passed all the other cars...

…and won!
My aunt was so happy, she jumped
up and down. I jumped, too.
I spilled my popcorn on the
lady in front of me.

We went over to the track to see
my uncle. He gave me and my aunt
a big kiss.

After they gave my uncle his trophy,
he drove me around the track one last time.

I held the checkered flag
up in the air.

When I got home, I showed Mom
and Dad the trophy. My uncle said
I could keep it until the next day.

I was so tired, I wanted to go to bed,
but I was too dirty.

Mom made me take a bath.

I fell asleep in the tub.

Mom put me to bed and kissed me good night. I hope I can go to the races again soon.